THE WHITE STORK IN THE SKY

Stories by Byelorussian Writers

RADUGA PUBLISHERS

MOSCOW

Translated into English by *Sergei Sosinsky*
Edited by *Gill Parry*
Designed by *Mikhail Krakovsky*
Compiled by *Vladimir Lipsky*

БЕЛЫЙ АИСТ ЛЕТИТ...

Рассказы писателей Белоруссии

На английском языке

Printed in the Union of Soviet Socialist Republics

Перевод сделан по изданиям: сборники издательства «Детская литература», журнала «Веселка», издательства «Советский писатель».

Для младшего школьного возраста

Б $\dfrac{4803010000-130}{031(05)-85}$ 022-85

ISBN 5-05-000029-7

CONTENTS

Introduction

A LAND WITH BLUE EYES

The white stork in the sky o'er Polesie
Above green humid meads,
Byelorussian sweet tunes in the heathers
In the rustle of reeds...

People call lakes the eyes of the earth. In my Byelorussia, one of the Soviet Union's fifteen republics, there are about 11,000 lakes. They are as blue and as clear as dewdrops. They reflect your face like a mirror.

My republic's emblem features bright blue flax flowers. Imagine thousands of hectares of flax in blossom. So many blue eyes looking at the clear sky above my Byelorussia!

When you meet a Byelorussian, there is an even chance that he has blue eyes. Perhaps these eyes are a reflection of the blue lakes and rivers, of the blossoming flax and forget-me-nots, of the gentle blue sky? Perhaps it is the other way round. Perhaps, nature's beauty and tenderness comes from the warm eyes of kind people?

However it may be, blue colour makes people feel happy, puts them in a good mood and makes them smile.

But the Byelorussian sky was not always clear and blue. It burned with the flames of war. The blue lakes and rivers ran red with blood. We bound the bloody wounds with bandages made of flax.

The Nazi barbarians inflicted desolation on my republic.One in four of my people died during the Second World War. The forces of occupation burned and razed 209 towns and cities and 9,200 villages.

The grim bells of the Byelorussian village of Khatyn resound worldwide. In 1943 the Nazis razed it to the ground and exterminated its entire population, old men, women and babies: of the 149 people who died there 76 were children. Today on the site of Khatyn stands a tragic monument to freedom-loving Byelorussians.

Byelorussia has another world-famous monument: the Hero Fortress of Brest which stands proud and unconquered to this day. The museum has stones inscribed with the words, "We'll die but never surrender!"

People united in friendship, common aims and concerns cannot be conquered. We aim to build the kindest society on earth, and our main concern is that the people in our country and, indeed, in every country live in peace under a clear blue sky.

Today, my Byelorussia has blossomed into a wonderful bouquet of flowers. The wounded earth has been nursed to health by the farmers' careful hands. Grain ripens in the fields, gardens yield plentiful fruit, cattle graze in rich pastures and lakes are blue again.

Byelorussians, those age-old tillers of the soil, have learned how to make high quality computers, heavy duty lorries, tractors, watches, refrigerators, and colour TV sets.

The bowels of the earth have revealed their mysteries. Completely new occupations have appeared in the republic: oil drillers, miners and gas prospectors.

But our pride and joy are the children, they are our hope for the future. They get the best the republic has to offer. The best buildings for kindergartens, schools, and Young Pioneer palaces. They get the best toys, books and songs. In return we expect them to grow up to be a credit to their country.

The stories in this book were written by modern Byelorussian authors. It tells about Byelorussian children. The authors represent different generations. Yanka Bryl is Byelorussia's veteran writer. Vasil Vitka's works have received the International Andersen Diploma. Alyona Vasilevich has won the State Prize.

They offer their short stories in the sincere hope that they will help young readers in other countries to learn more about life in the Soviet Union and about the Soviet people's desire for peace.

Vladimir Lipsky,
editor of the Byelorussian children's
magazine *Vyaselka*

Yanka Bryl

LINDA AND LITTLE MAPLE

For my daughter Galya

1

The roadman's little green house stands next to the motorway.

From a passing car all one can glimpse are the green walls and a fence, also green, the white surrounds on the large windows and a motley-coloured tiled roof. Further along the road come rows of saplings recently planted by the roadside, telegraph poles, fields and forests.

Little four-year-old Linda lives in this attractive house which stands all by itself along the road.

Linda loves standing by the roadside, waving her hands at every passing car and urging her best friend, the fatty old dog Rick, to bark at it. Once Linda gave in to the temptation, spat on her palms like the boys do and started running to the opposite side of the very wide asphalt strip, smooth as a table. Before she had reached the middle of the road a motorcar tooted its horn twice. Her little bare feet grew numb with fear. Linda stopped in her tracks and burst out crying: "Mummy!" The car stopped, and the driver opened his door to scold her. But Rick barked so fiercely at him that Uncle Driver shut the door and drove off in fright.

Since then little Linda has not dared to cross the road without Mummy and Daddy. And she very rarely stands near the road now. Only on days when she hears a big, smudgy tractor crawl like a caterpillar with a deafening rumbling.

2

Mother and Father went into town. In the evening, Mother came home alone, bringing a long-awaited gift: a little fur coat.

Mother dressed up her Goldilocks and fastened all the buttons on the fur coat. Then she lifted the little girl in her arms, turned her towards the lamp and exclaimed with admiration:

"Why, you're my Snow White!"

Linda immediately forgot that she had been upset because Father would not be home until tomorrow. She wanted to go for a walk in her new fur coat. But Mother said it was too late today: the night was drawing in and it was freezing cold. Linda grizzled a little, but then calmed down. All right, she would wait until tomorrow but, please, would Mother allow her to wear the fur coat all evening. Mother laughed and said yes. But it was very warm at home: Grandmother, dreading the cold, had burned a huge pile of birch wood in the stove. Linda soon threw off her new fur coat and went to bed patiently waiting for the new day to come.

She lay for a while, pondering, and then asked:

"Mummy, isn't it too cold for Little Maple today?"

3

The maple sapling grew on the other side of the road Linda was not supposed to cross. It was not alone, for many other saplings had been planted last autumn along the road, maples, lindens and birches. There were even four apple and pear saplings. They grew right beside the maple Linda had planted.

How could a little girl have planted a tree all by herself? Well, she did not really do it by herself, she held the little maple upright in the hole, while two boys filled it with earth.

The boys were called Vladik and Alex. Then there were Mikhas, Marylka, Maya and Olya. A whole school of children!

At first Linda stood at the open gate and watched them planting trees from across the motorway. Listening to the murmur of children's voices, shaggy Rick raised his head, screwed up his eyes and cheerfully tapped the gate with his tail. Linda wanted to join the children so much!

The children seemed to realise it because they went up to the edge of the road and shouted:

"Little girl, does your dog bite?"

"No, our Rick doesn't bite children," cried Linda standing on tiptoe.

"Come here then! Help us plant trees!"

The two boys, Vladik and Alex, ran across the road, took Linda by the hand and, looking nervously first at the big shaggy dog running after the girl and then at the hill from over which a car might appear any moment, walked carefully across the road.

The teacher who was further on with another group of children told the boys off at first for bringing the little girl here without asking her mother or father. But then she picked Linda up, talked to her, and kissed her on both cheeks just like Mother.

The children chose the smallest and prettiest maple sapling for Linda.

Now it stands in the open, tied to a pole. It holds on to the pole with its straw arm like a little child that cannot walk alone yet. And it's so cold outside and there's so much snow!

"Mummy, when can I go and look at the maple?" asked Linda.

4

A hare hopped carefully over the firm showdrifts at dawn. Sensing the hare, Rick, who was resting on the doorstep of the green house, pricked up his ears, growled angrily and finally barked out loud: Woof! Woof! Woof!

The frightened hare jumped up, scurried away and flew over the snowdrifts like an arrow.

In the morning Rick followed the hare's twisted trail around the house and the garden, and then disappeared. When he returned, Linda Snow White, wearing her white fur coat, was standing in the open gateway joyfully screwing up her eyes against the bright sun.

Rick came up to Snow White and, as usual, brushed against her, pushing his head under her little hand as if saying: "Hallo, Linda! Please pat me and stroke my long ears."

"Go away, you," said Linda, pursing her lips. "You'll get my coat dirty. Go away!"

Taking her hand out of the soft white muff, she pushed him away.

"So that's how you feel!" Rick said, not offended at all. "And I wanted to show you something."

At this point Rick suddenly jumped up with a joy known only to himself, began to spin, flattened himself on the ground and barked: Woof! Woof! Woof!

Linda laughed and ran after him through the clean sparkling snow.

5

This time it was Rick's fault that Linda disobeyed her parents and crossed the motorway alone once again. He ran to the other side and began calling her: Woof! Woof! Woof!

The sun, the new fur coat and the snow were also to blame. She felt so merry, so warm, so good! Linda thought for a moment, looked back and, taking her hands out of her muff, began to run. Crossing the deep iced tracks on the road, she fell, her warm hands first. At first she was frightened—the snow tickled and burned!—then she laughed and cried out:

"Rick! Wait, doggy, I'm coming!"

Instead of waiting for his little friend, Rick went back for her and they raced on together. They crossed the motorway and found themselves on a narrow byroad with trees planted along it, and then Linda remembered something, stopped and said:

"Rick, Little Maple's there! Over there! Silly doggy, you don't even know..."

Linda stood on a hard road well trodden in by horses, while Rick was behind the trees in deep snow.

"Let's go this way, doggy, over here!" Snow White cried.

But Rick was up to mischief again: the alluring, exciting trail of the hare ran before him. They were the same tracks that had led him so far into the field, almost up to the forest, the same hare that had circled outside their house the night before.

"Woof! Woof! Woof!" Rick barked. In doggy language this meant: "It's better to go this way!"

Linda took no notice of him, and ran along the byroad. When she reached the place where she'd planted the maple she turned off the road, and ran over the snow crust. Then she fell, her warm hands touching the snow again. But she did not cry this time either. As she got up, she shouted:

"Little Maple, how are you?"

6

One after another tears as big as pearls rolled from Snow White's blue eyes. Then more and more came.

Normally, Linda would not have cried: she was no cry-baby! But some cruel person had broken two of the saplings. Not the maple, but the apple saplings, which Olya and Alex had planted. Not really broken them, but peeled the bark off the trunk and broken off all the little branches.

Rick wagged his tail to calm Linda down. He shifted his weight from one paw to the other and howled softly. But how could Rick make the girl understand that the blame lay with that bad, mean hare and Grandmother. She had not got up during the night to open the door and let Rick out. Instead she'd only banged angrily on the wall for him to stop barking. Now see what has happened!

At first Rick growled, then angry at the hare began to bark: Woof! Woof! "Just wait, Long Ears, I'll get you!" Rick scolded the hare in doggy language. But Linda could not understand him.

At last, she stopped crying, wiped her eyes with her cold little fists, hid her hands inside the muff and said just as Father would, quite like an adult:

"Rick, follow me!"

She carefully stepped off the snow onto the road, and looked around again to see whether Mummy or Grannie were around. Then, without hurrying she walked not home but towards the place where the farm schoolhouse had only recently been built.

Rick followed Linda. This time he behaved himself, he didn't turn off the road or run ahead once.

7

On a chilly, clear night a sled would rustle by or a car would dash past along the motorway. A bell jingling on a shaft-bow could be heard far away and the roar from a car engine carried even further. Sitting in the warm car or running after the sled to warm themselves people smoked, talked and laughed.

Meanwhile, Linda Snow White was asleep in the quiet green house by the roadside.

The new fur coat and the muff were hanging in the closet. Rick was dozing in the passage. He growled angrily in his sleep, apparently remembering something unpleasant, then cocked an ear listening whether the long-eared scoundrel who had ruined the apple saplings was making his way through the snow.

And Linda was asleep.

She dreamed that the hare had gone to the saplings again and wanted to nibble at the two apple trees Olya and Vladik had planted. But they were all dressed in soft straw coats. Linda had gone to the school, and the children came and tied straw round the apple trees. Then the hare decided to gnaw at Linda's maple sapling to punish her for having gone to the school. But the maple was also in a straw coat. Linda asked the schoolchildren to protect her nice Little Maple. Let it have a coat too, it's just as little as Linda. The hare tried to reach at the branch. Little Maple like a boy who can't walk yet clapped its branches, that were like Linda's hands, and laughed gaily.

Linda laughed too. She was being taken across the motorway again on a sled just as she had been in the daytime. Alex, Vladik and Olya were pulling the sled. Very many children: a whole school! Rick ran along with them, barking merrily: Woof! Woof! Then the lady teacher picked Linda up, passed her over to her mother and said.

"Don't be angry with Linda, she had to come and see us. Today Linda was a good girl!"

Little Maple was still laughing and clapping its hands.

Vasil Vitka

A DIFFICULT FRIENDSHIP

There are hotheads like that: you could bang his head against a brick wall and all he'd do is grin.

They say it's no good talking to boys like that.

I heard about just such a hothead in Yelnichi, my home town.

Yevstrat Skachilias was rarely ever seen during the daytime. A mild elderly man, he had worked for many years as night watchman on a farm. Even on warm summer nights Yevstrat would don a winter coat and a fur hat with one of its ear flaps hanging down to his collar, while the other stuck out as if listening attentively to the quiet. He would leave his house with a gun slung over his shoulder.

Although he was not talkative he could not resist going up to a group of people talking among themselves, and would stand and listen to them. Sometimes he would even put in a word or two of his own and then disappear into the night as quietly as he had come.

No one in Yelnichi could say anything nasty about Yevstrat or about three of his sons. However, the fourth and youngest, Yuzik, was such a tearaway, that no one could understand who he's taken after.

Perhaps it was because the youngest child in the family always gets more attention and becomes spoiled. Yuzik did just as he pleased and acknowledged no one's authority.

The brat seemed barely knee-high, yet when he started going to school, he became the terror of his form. He'd thump his classmates on the back, grab a book from a bag and tear it to pieces or get up to some other mischief.

You had to keep your eyes on that good-for-nothing all the time.

Neither tears nor threats helped.

The teacher complained to his father, but Yevstrat was soft with his youngest son. He had to go to the school so many times to make excuses for his son, but never would he punish Yuzik, instead he tried to reason with the boy. Yuzik pretended to listen to his father, but as soon as he was at large, he'd be at his tricks again.

No one knows how long this would have gone on if it were not for something that aroused the whole village.

The school had just broken up for the summer.

The best time of the year began. The trees had such rich foliage on their long branches that it was difficult to see from below what was happening at the top.

It was at the top of the poplar tree, which stood across the street from Yevstrat's house, that very important events were taking place.

Just before the beginning of spring Yevstrat's neighbour, Adam Patrubeika, and his son Tolik hoisted an old wheel to the top of the tree. Tolik wanted storks to come and live in the poplar.

The birds did not disappoint Tolik. They flew into the tree, made a nest and settled down. They trusted people, and often circled low over the house, and even landed in the back yard.

From the street you could see them strutting among the chickens, glancing sideways at the quarrelsome cockerel who, for some reason, did not approve of such fraternising.

While these wise and kind newcomers were building their nest, bringing fledgelings into the world and then feeding them from morning to night, a friendship was struck up between Yuzik and Tolik.

This was unexpected, really, because only recently Yuzik and Tolik had been forever picking quarrels and rolling in the school yard during

break-time and then going into class after the bell with buttons torn off their clothes and sometimes even with blood streaming from their noses.

Now they couldn't live without each other for a day. It was the storks that brought them together.

The boys had grown very fond of those intelligent birds and watched them day after day.

At first, when the fledgelings were still small, the man stork and the lady stork used to fly out from the nest one at a time, but when the young storks grew bigger, they went together and still they couldn't bring enough food home for the family.

The boys laughed gleefully watching the four fledgelings, trying to stand at the edge of the nest, snuggling up together because they were frightened of the height. The parents were screeching warnings at them.

One day Yuzik said:

"Tolik, let's climb up to the nest and take one little stork for me and one for you."

Tolik didn't like the idea:

"No, we shouldn't. They'd die of hunger!"

"We'll feed them."

"How'll you feed them?" Tolik laughed. "Would you catch frogs in the swamp and bring them here?"

Yuzik couldn't bear anyone to laugh at him. He frowned and glared at Tolik.

"I know why you don't want to!" he exploded. "You think they're your storks? Yours? Now I'm going to throw the whole blasted wheel off the tree!" Reaching for the lower branch Yuzik pulled himself up easily and climbed up the rough tree trunk.

"I'm not going to let you!" cried out Tolik.

He ran up and tugged at Yuzik's shirt with all his might. Yuzik slid down, his face rubbing against the bark, and tumbled to the ground.

Jumping to his feet and feeling the pain in his scratched face, Yuzik clenched his fists, preparing to attack his former friend. But Tolik managed to dart into the house.

Yuzik heard the latch grate and the door was bolted right before his nose.

"You'll remember me, Patrubeichik!" the furious Yuzik threatened Tolik.

"Stupid fool!" Tolik shouted boldly from behind the door and went upstairs to the attic.

There, he looked out of the little round window facing the street, and waited to see what Yuzik would do.

He did not have to wait long.

Yuzik dashed home. Through the little window Tolik could see Yuzik rush in through the door and come out again almost immediately.

He was carrying a gun. Not the toy one carved out of wood which they played guerrillas with only recently, but the real thing, which Yevstrat Skachilias carried to his job as night watchman.

This was so unexpected that Tolik was at a complete loss: what did the fool intend to do?

Coming out of the gate Yuzik stopped, raised the gun and aimed it—guess where? At the very roof window of Patrubeika's house, where Tolik was hiding.

"Aaah!" Tolik screamed in terror and fled headlong from the attic into the house. "Dad, dearest! Yuzik wants to shoot me!" he blurted out, when the shot rang out. A frightened cry came from Yevstrat's wife, Yuzik's mother:

"What did you do that for, Yuzik? Did Tolik bother you? Did he cut you off from the sunlight? Oh, woe me!"

Unable to understand what had happened, Tolik's father stared at his son in astonishment.

"He missed me!" Tolik cried out happily and rushing from the house into the yard shouted to Yuzik's mother: "He didn't kill me, Aunt Nastya!"

At that very moment, he caught sight of Yuzik. The other boy was standing at the fence, looking very pale, his head drooping. The gun lay at his feet. Tolik felt so sorry for his friend that he had to say something:

"Yuzik..." he called quietly.

Yuzik did not budge.

"How can you feel sorry for that rascal?" Tolik heard a woman neighbour say, reproaching him. Then he became aware that a whole crowd had gathered in the street under the windows of their house.

Tolik could hear anxious questions and angry replies:

"Who did it?"

"Yevstrat's brat, who else?"

"Oh, dear! How could he do such a thing?"

"Ask him. Look at him, glaring at everybody like a little wolf cub."

Tolik looked at Yuzik once again.

His heart ached with sympathy.

He couldn't understand why the people were so angry with Yuzik. "Well, maybe he did want to kill me when he was angry. But he's suffering now, poor fellow."

Tolik turned to the crowd and wanted to cry out: "Here I am. Look, I'm alive!" but the words stuck in his throat.

What he saw in that short instant was too dreadful for words. It was even worse than his worst fears.

The people stepped aside.

The stork lay in the middle of the street. Its legs, now blue, were tucked underneath its body, its long neck stretched out, wings spread out as if it was trying to rise up. But it could not.

The bird was dead.

Tolik felt the street sway. Big dark circles floated in front of him.

He huddled up so as not to fall, he felt very small and helpless, and also cold, as if it were winter and not a hot summer.

He did not remember his father leading him into the house, he did not hear people saying that when Yuzik rushed out with the gun he himself did not know what he intended to do. He just wanted to get back at Tolik. Seeing the stork flying over Patrubeika's house he aimed and riddled the stork with a whole charge of bird-shot.

The street buzzed like a beehive.

The people scolded and reproached Yevstrat and Nastya Skachilias, and some openly declared that there was no place for a troublemaker like their son in Yelnichi and that they could only expect trouble from such a ruffian.

Meanwhile Yuzik had disappeared.

Emotions were running so high that the people did not at once notice the commotion that had started in the clear summer sky.

Not just one bereaved mother stork but a whole flock had learned of the tragedy and were now screeching in grief and despair above Patrubeika's old poplar.

The little storks were standing hungry in the nest huddling together in fright.

The troubled storks were now flying right above the people's heads. They must have flown here from all the nests in the neighbourhood.

As soon as the people went away, the storks landed in the street. They surrounded the dead bird, and their sorrowful screams did not subside for a long time.

Faces pressed against windowpanes. The scene was taking place in front of Tolik's house. Soon, his mother could bear it no longer. She ran out and wailed:

"People, neighbours, something has to be done..."

Yevstrat Skachilias came out of his yard with a spade. The adults and children came out of other houses.

The storks flapped their wings, took off and began to circle in the air again.

Skachilias approached the dead bird, stuck his spade in the roadside turf and began to dig a hole.

Everyone saw that the quiet Yevstrat felt the tragedy acutely. He was angry with his son, and was prepared to take this last sad duty upon himself, so as to make at least some amends before the people and before his conscience.

22

"My dear Yevstrat!" Tolik's mother flung up her hands. "What are you up to? It's not a very neighbourly thing to do."

Skachilias stopped digging. He couldn't understand what he'd done to offend his neighbour.

"It'll be in front of our windows for ever and ever. Do we deserve such punishment?" Tolik's mother started crying.

Everyone agreed: it would have been unfair.

Yevstrat stood for a while, thinking. He looked at the crowd, bent over the stork, lifted it up, took the spade and headed for the end of his garden.

The people followed Skachilias through his yard.

Yevstrat buried the stork near some cherry trees.

The grief-stricken birds, now silent, wandered through Yevstrat's garden for a long time, oblivious of the people and clawing at the fresh mound in despair.

Towards evening two baby storks fell out of the nest. They were not fully fledged yet.

It was difficult to say whether it was sorrow that caused this to happen or whether they had become weak from not eating for a whole day. Most probably, the mother stork, realising that she would be unable to feed the whole family alone, had left them to die.

But the baby storks were still alive. When Tolik brought them into the house, gave them some millet gruel and then put them into a place behind the stove and covered them with a coat, they perked up and began to tug at his sleeve with their little beaks.

When everyone was asleep in the Patrubeika household, Yuzik's mother tapped on the window.

"Tolik!" she called in a troubled voice.

Tolik jumped from his bed and ran into the yard.

"Tolik, my dear. Our Yuzik's gone, and we don't know where to look for him. Father's been everywhere..."

Tolik went back into the house and lit a lamp.

Yevstrat's wife rushed to her house again.

She walked barefoot around the big boulder lying near the porch, crying and complaining quietly.

"Oh, when will the daytime finally come... I've been to see everyone... My dear boy, my precious," she began crying louder when she saw Tolik with the lamp. "I just hope he doesn't think of something terrible... Now I'll go and ask the neighbours again, maybe I'll learn something..." And she disappeared into the night along the street.

Tolik walked through Yevstrat's yard.

Seriously worried about Yuzik's disappearance, he remembered the impulsive Yuzik's guilty face as he stood in front of the people that day. A sense of duty to a friend even though it was a difficult, offended friendship compelled Tolik to set out on a night search without wasting a moment.

The first thing Tolik did was to climb into the attic of Yevstrat's house.

At the window under the roof Yuzik had obviously stood for a long time. A bundle of last year's straw had turned into dust under his feet.

So Yuzik had heard and seen everything that had happened in the street and in their yard.

Coming down from the attic Tolik walked out into the yard lighting his way with the lamp.

Frightened and uncertain, he paused at the well, but, nervous about looking into its dark inside, opened the light wicket gate and moved along a furrow towards the end of the garden.

Knocking the cold dew from the potato tops, he soon reached the place where Yevstrat had buried the stork.

The lamp's bright light fell on a clearing by the cherry trees.

Yes, Yuzik was here.

He sat huddled on the packed darkened mound, while the mother-stork stood not far from him in the furrow. Her head stuck out above the tall potato tops. Tolik saw the stork close her eyes to the bright light for an instant and then open them again. Her eyes were sad and reproachful.

Yuzik did not budge.

Bending towards him, Tolik saw that the boy was motionless, as if frozen still. Perhaps he was asleep? But Tolik had never seen anyone sleep sitting up before.

It was a hard hour in his friend's life. He had taken his first look into his own soul, which he himself did not understand, which had led him astray, and he could no longer shrug off his profound feeling of guilt and forget all that had happened.

Tolik touched his friend's shoulder.

Yuzik said nothing.

Then Tolik grabbed him by the elbow and pulled him with all his might.

Yuzik rose. Shifting his feet uncertainly, like a baby trying to take its first steps, he followed Tolik obediently.

They walked in silence along the furrow and then through the yard to Skachilias' house.

At the threshold, Yuzik said in a voice that could barely be heard:

"What'll happen now, Tolik?"

"I don't know."

They both stood in silence for a long time. Then Tolik lifted the glass cover of the lamp and blew out the light. The early dawn was breaking through the cherry trees.

"Did she stand there all night like that?"

"All night," Yuzik bowed his head in shame.

"I have two baby storks behind the stove. They fell out of the nest," said Tolik. "Now we'll have to take care of them until they grow up."

"Yes, we will," Yuzik agreed.

Yadviga Beganskaya

MYSTERIOUS- HELPERS

The frost had drawn pretty patterns on the windows, scattering merry lights of different colours. The wind was blowing outside, swaying the branches and howling down the chimney.

"Grannie, tell us a story," asked Olya brushing against Grandmother's warm hand.

"Only make it a happy story, Grannie, so that the wind stops howling and we will have sweet dreams," said Tolik huddling close to Grandmother and looking fondly into her eyes.

Grandmother put aside her needlework, lifted her glasses up to her forehead, and a kind smile lit up her fine wrinkles.

"Which story should I tell you?" she asked smoothing the tuft of hair that so stubbornly stuck up on Tolik's head. "I'll tell you about the little magic people. Now listen."

"Once upon a time there lived a shoemaker," Grandmother started her story, "who became so poor that he had only one small piece of leather left. 'I'll cut the leather now to make a pair of shoes and tomorrow I'll sew them,' the shoemaker decided and went to bed. In the morning when he got up to start work he found a pair of shoes standing on his bench ready. They were the most beautiful shoes he'd ever seen. The shoemaker sold the shoes and bought some more leather with the money. Then he cut it up for four pairs of shoes. In the morning he got up and found that the four pairs of shoes were ready. This went on for some time. It didn't matter how much leather the shoemaker cut in the evening—the shoes would be ready in the morning. 'I'd like to see who sews these shoes for me every night,' the shoemaker wondered. That night he hid behind the stove and waited. At midnight, two little elves appeared, sat down at the bench and began to sew the shoes. They disappeared as soon as they'd finished."

That evening Grandmother told the children lots of interesting things about the magic elves. What Olya and Tolik liked most was that these little people helped the big people without being seen.

"Grannie, would you like to have helpers like them?" asked Tolik.

"Of course I would, dear," said Grandmother and began to sew again.

"It's a pity they only live in stories, or they'd write the letter 'g' for me. It doesn't look right when I do it," Tolik sighed.

"Now you must go to sleep," said Grandmother. "That story's made us so late."

Lying in her bed, Olya looked at the windows lit up by the moon and thought about the little magic people. "What if Tolik and I..."

Olya smiled, propped herself up in bed and called her brother softly.

"Tolik, eh Tolik, are you asleep?"

"No."

"Do you know what I've been thinking?"

"What?"

"Let's pretend we're little people too."

"How?" Tolik was surprised.

"Come here and we'll talk. Only quietly so Grannie doesn't hear."

In a flash Tolik was already sitting with his sister on her bed. No one knows what they talked about.

In the morning Grandmother got up and was just about to go outside for some firewood when she saw the wood lying next to the stove. She decided to go to the well for water, but the water was already in the house: a full pail stood on the bench, its bluish eye gazing at her. Grandmother went to the porch and stared in disbelief: someone had swept the snow from

28

the paths and scattered sand on them so they wouldn't be slippery. She went to milk the cow, and while she was there, someone cleared the table and swept the floor.

Grandmother only shook her head in surprise and smiled, while Olya and Tolik stole glances at her and winked at each other. Olya had certainly invented a very interesting game.

Grandmother was delighted to have little magic people helping her. It made the housework much easier. When Mother and Father returned, Grandmother told them everything.

"How can we thank the little magic people for their work?" asked Mother, glancing at Olya and Tolik.

"Just a moment! I've got two oranges. I was going to give them to the children, but I think it'd be better to leave them for the little people," said Father, pulling two big golden oranges from the bag.

"But, Dad, it's..." Tolik cried, running towards his father, but Olya tugged his arm so hard he stopped immediately.

"What did you say, son?" Father asked, pretending not to notice.

"He wanted to ask how you're going to give the little people the oranges if you don't know where they are?" Olya came to her brother's rescue.

"Well, we won't look for them. We'll just put the oranges on a plate and leave them on the table. When the little people come they'll realise that this is a gift for their work," said Grandmother, smiling.

The oranges were delicious, juicy and fragrant. Olya and Tolik ate them and left the peelings on the plate and put the plate back on the table. Let Grandmother think that her little helpers had eaten the treat.

"We'll pretend we're little magic people again tomorrow, won't we?" inquired Tolik as he went to bed that evening.

"Of course we will," said Olya. "I'll teach Natasha, Ira, Nadia and all my friends to play the game."

"And I'll teach my classmates," said Tolik.

Ales Makhnach,
participant in the defence of the Brest Fortress

CHILDREN OF THE BREST FORTRESS

It was the first week of a great and terrible war. Hitler's advance units had already reached the approaches to Minsk,* while two Nazi infantry divisions were still battling for the Brest Fortress.

Enemy generals and officers were in a quandary. How could they destroy the little border garrison? Then they decided: they would force the Russians to surrender from hunger and thirst. They would do everything

---

* Minsk is the capital of Byelorussia.

they could to exhaust the defenders as quickly as possible, but the most important thing was to leave the Soviet soldiers without water. Then the heavy machine-guns would no longer fire, the fortress defenders would weaken from thirst and it would be easy to destroy them.

The Nazis took heart from the plan and dug in around the fortress, training their sights on every stone, every bush, and every machine-gun nest, particularly those along the banks of the Zapadny Bug and its tributary, the Mukhovets. The fortress was sprayed with large-calibre shells and a hail of armour-piercing, incendiary and explosive bullets. The enemy sent in heavy tanks, and aircraft, used flame-throwers, and tear gas and kept storming the Soviet positions.

It was very tough on the defenders of the fortress.

The infirmary chief, Natalya Konstrovskaya, complained:

"We've no medicines and no bandages. The number of the wounded increases with every battle."

"Many people are lying dead in Citadel Square. They probably all have first aid kits," said Nyura, the fifteen-year-old daughter of the frontier post commander Andrei Kizhevatov.

"You can't reach them. That place is under heavy fire."

"Heavy fire won't stop me," retorted Valya Henkina, Nyura's friend.

When bandages appeared in the infirmary, Natalya refused to believe her eyes. Apparently, the girls had crept out of the cellar at night to the square which was riddled with shellholes. It was the scene of bitter fighting during the day.

The regiment's ward Kolya Novikov could not keep quiet when he heard about this feat and blurted out his secret:

"Doctor, we'll be treating you to some sweets soon."

"Yes, we're going to bring some!" Petya Vasilyev confirmed his friend's words.

Everyone took it as a joke. Where on earth would they find any sweets? People had not seen a crust of bread for days.

But the schoolchildren were certainly not joking. They climbed up to the first floor of the circular barracks building from where they studied the way to the place where a shop had once stood. Before the war it had sold various household goods and food stuffs. Now it lay in ruins. Soon the regiment's children headed for no man's land, the place between the Soviet-held barracks and the Nazi positions, crawling on all fours or dashing from one shellhole to the next.

"Come back!" yelled the soldiers.

But the children were already far away. They didn't hear the cries, or perhaps they did but refused to take any notice.

Half an hour passed. The schoolchildren appeared in the infirmary with a gas mask packed full and a bale of pretty cotton fabric.

"You went there in broad daylight?!" Valya said with surprise and reproach.

"We wouldn't have found all this at night," answered Kolya pointing to the bag with biscuits and sweets.

They treated other children and the badly wounded. The doctor, Nyura and Valya weren't left out either.

"You've left nothing for yourselves," remarked the doctor.

"We're neither little children nor wounded," fourteen-year-old Petya Klypa answered for everyone.

The doctor and the girls decided to give their treats to the little children.

There was a gift for the women, too: the cotton fabric, which could be used to make pretty dresses.

However, the women were not thinking about new dresses: they began to tear up the fabric for bandages.

Lieutenant Kizhevatov ordered the regiment's wards to be confined to the infirmary for combat operations undertaken without permission. Thus the children came under the command of women. Even so, the boys managed to sneak out of the infirmary, especially when fighting raged above. But they didn't tell anyone where they had been and what they had done.

It was dark and stuffy in the overcrowded infirmary. The badly wounded kept asking for water.

The little children were also crying constantly for water and calling: "Mummy, Mummy..."

The little medical orderlies tried to cheer up and comfort the smaller children.

"There'll be water at night!" Kolya Novikov promised firmly.

Towards evening Kolya spoke anxiously to Petya Vasilyev:

"Did you hear what I said? I promised for the two of us."

Petya said nothing.

"I'm talking about water," Kolya insisted. "We have to go to the Mukhovets tonight..."

"I was thinking that too," said Petya without raising his head.

Soon the boys were crouching behind the ruined barracks wall. Kolya spoke first:

"Looks like Hitler himself has ordered the banks to be covered by heavy fire. To us water is..."

"...like gold," Volodya Izmailov continued.

"Even more precious!" the twelve-year-old Petya Kotelnikov corrected him.

"Quiet!" Kolya hushed the boys. "You can't buy water here for all the gold in the world. Petya and I have a good plan. Hitler will die before he sees through it! We must crawl in between the dead Nazis, then if we're spotted by a searchlight or flare they won't notice that we're alive."

Kolya showed the boys what to do.

"We must crawl slowly and smoothly like a turtle," he taught the boys. "Then the flasks won't make any noise and everyone will think there's just another dead Nazi on the bank."

"Boys, what about the flasks?" Nyura Kizhevatova remembered.

"We have to look for them before it gets dark!" Valya Henkina added.

"There's plenty of time!" retorted Petya.

"We should look for them while it's still light," Kolya supported the girls.

"We can do it now," Petya Vasilyev finally agreed. "But they must be wrapped up in cloth and have corks that screw on tightly. It'll take us all of half an hour to crawl the fifty meters."

When it was quite dark, the regiment's boys set out on their difficult mission. Nyura and Valya saw them off.

"Maybe we should tell our soldiers after all. So they know you're there and don't fire at you—it's dark, you know," Nyura tried to persuade the boys.

"Of all the stupid ideas!" Kolya fumed.

"Not a word to anyone!" Volodya Izmailov warned the girls.

"You don't know anything about the mission! Got it?" said Stepan Aksyonov.

"Say nothing about the mission. It's top secret!" Petya Vasilyev concluded after a pause.

Nyura and Valya were afraid for them. "Boys! Don't go! You might be killed!" the girls were on the point of hurling these words into the troubled night, where darkness was broken now and again by searchlights sharp as razors and flares bursting above the river and flooding its banks with light.

The boys of the Brest Fortress couldn't turn back now. They had given their word, a Young Pioneer's word, that they would get water.

Before Nyura's eyes stood her little brother Vanya and little sister Galya, begging Grandmother, Mother and Nyura:

"I want something to drink! Water!"

Nor could she forget the Nazis' fierce attack this morning. She could still hear the desperate cry from frontier guard Grisha Yeremeyev:

"Men! Water! The last water in the machine gun is boiling!"

No! The girls wouldn't shout at the boys to come back. The Young Pioneer girls would wait for them to return from this truly heroic mission. Both Valya and Nyura believed that the boys would all come back alive. Then the girls would take the flasks in the cellar and tell everyone eagerly:

"Our people fetched it from the Mukhovets!"

"Who are these heroes?" the defenders would want to know. "Who managed to reach the stream and return?"

"We don't know. Some soldiers came during the night. But it was dark and we couldn't see who it was," Nyura and Valya would answer in unison.

In the morning Lieutenant Kizhevatov would inspect the positions and drop in to the infirmary as usual. All the previous night's events would be reported to the commander. The regiment's boys would also report— Volodya would do it for them all.

"We're staying in the cellar carrying out your orders, Comrade Lieutenant. We're helping to care for the wounded and the children!" he would say.

The lieutenant would notice Kolya's bandaged head and inquire anxiously:

"What happened?"

"Oh, it's nothing!" the boy would answer with a smile, overcoming pain. "I walked into an iron bar in the cellar last night."

The lieutenant would never know who had dared go to the river, from which few had returned alive lately.

No one, except Nyura and Valya, would know that the heroes were the regiment's children. And Kolya's bruise from an "iron bar" was really a bullet wound he received that night.

Alyona Vasilevich

LEAFLET, THE PARTISAN HORSE

Leaflet was the name of a young bay horse. This was because she had a square white spot on her forehead exactly like a leaflet. In this short story I'm going to tell you how this horse joined the partisans.

In the early months of the war Leaflet was wounded in the leg by a splinter from a grenade. Although the wound was serious, Leaflet's master, a young cavalryman, could not bring himself to shoot her, so he left her to be cared for by an old peasant in the village for which the battle had been.

"I can't do it. She's almost human, understands every word," said the soldier sadly to the peasant, patting Leaflet's downcast head. "Take good care of her, old man. She might pull through. Then she'll be useful to you."

Leaflet listened to her master, nuzzled her silky head gently against his hand, and her intelligent eyes expressed endless sorrow.

"Stay alive and healthy yourself, lad. Don't worry about the horse. I'll look after her," the peasant assured the cavalryman.

"Thanks, old man," the soldier shook his hand firmly and ran off to catch up with his troop.

So Leaflet had a new master. And she was very fortunate, indeed. The peasant was kind and considerate, he looked after Leaflet and treated her wound as best he could. She soon recovered from the wound, only dragged her right back leg a little. And by autumn even that was gone.

It was on a wet autumn night that partisans tapped on the window of Leaflet's new master. One of them had to get to the next village as quickly as possible. So the old peasant led Leaflet out of the shed. The horse neighed shrilly, pawed the ground with her hoof, but, sensing that the reigns were held by a firm hand, obediently followed the partisan out of the yard.

That was when Leaflet joined the fighting partisans. The horse was amazingly intelligent, but she was also temperamental. If she didn't like a rider, she wouldn't carry him. She would neigh angrily and gnaw at her bit, rearing and circling in one place on her hind legs. Or while crossing a river during the march, she might suddenly lie down in the water.

Some of the more hot-tempered fellows disliked Leaflet and she got quite a few kicks from them. But she refused to submit. She blew into her nostrils and stamped the ground with her hoof.

Yet how well-behaved and obedient she could be if a person was gentle with her. Eventually, for some unknown reason, Leaflet singled out Tanya, a messenger, from the entire unit. Tanya had a thick braid of dark hair that reached down to her knee (several times she had concealed hand grenades in her hair and carried them through German and police posts) and twinkling grey eyes. Her laughter was like the jingling of silver bells. When Leaflet heard her laugh, she would prick up her short pointed ears and listen. Then she would neigh in joyful welcome.

It was a sincere and selfless friendship. Leaflet knew how to hide herself when necessary. She would lie on the ground without budging until permitted to rise. She could step soundlessly like a cat, and she cantered easily and swiftly. More than once Leaflet carried the fearless partisan girl away from enemy bullets. And Tanya, in return, often gave her comrade-in-arms the last crust of bread.

This is what happened to them once.

Mounted on Leaflet Tanya was returning from a combat mission along a forest road. Exhausted after a sleepless night Tanya dozed off. There were several kilometres to go before they reached the camp, but clever Leaflet knew all the partisan routes so there was no fear of losing her way. Suddenly Leaflet stopped. Tanya woke up to find the horse standing quite

still. She touched the horse with a stirrup—no response. Leaflet just wiggled her pricked-up ears. Tanya jerked the reigns—Leaflet still didn't move, didn't even turn her head, only shifted her legs restlessly as if saying: "Don't trouble me."

"Something's wrong," Leaflet communicated her anxiety to Tanya. The girl rose in the saddle and gently patted the horse's head.

Leaflet shuddered nervously, moved her ears again, listening intently to something. Then Tanya dismounted and headed for the bushes, at which Leaflet had been staring. The horse also took a few steps to follow her. Pushing aside the bushes Tanya went on. Leaflet followed her. Tanya's excitement mounted. Her sleepiness was gone. Now she could also sense a strange mixture of smells: burned leather, petrol and something else.

Feeling for her pistol in the pocket of her quilted jacket, Tanya pushed aside the bushes carefully and moved farther and farther from the road. Walking as noiselessly as Tanya, Leaflet did not lag behind a single step. Suddenly Tanya heard a weak groan. She backed away in surprise. Then, another groan. She couldn't make out any words. The person seemed very weak. Perhaps he was calling for help, perhaps asking for water...

Taking herself under control, Tanya whispered an order to the horse: "Leaflet, stay here!"

Taking her pistol in her right hand she moved towards the sound of the groans.

Another bush, yet another one: Tanya froze. The remains of a plane were smoking in a small clearing. A man was lying among the debris. It was a Soviet pilot.

The pilot's clothes were burned. He had lost consciousness from the burns and severe pain. Tanya tried to pull him into a sitting position, but he just let out a long groan and slumped to the ground again lifeless. Something had to be done, as quickly as possible.

Tanya remembered her faithful Leaflet. The clever animal was with her mistress in a flash after hearing her call.

"Leaflet, dear, help me!"

The horse listened to Tanya's anxious voice and obediently carried out all her orders.

She lowered herself down on the ground, her back turned to the pilot, and raised her head so that Tanya could tie the pilot's arms to her neck. Then Leaflet rose from the ground gently and waited for the girl to mount her. Then she set out for camp stepping ever so carefully.

From the partisan unit, the pilot was sent by plane to a Soviet hospital.

After the war the pilot happened to meet Tanya at Tushino Airport in Moscow. He recognised Tanya, was overjoyed and took her to meet his mates.

"Please meet Tanya, the partisan. She saved my life during the war," said the pilot.

"Oh, it wasn't me. It was Leaflet who did it. She heard..."

"It's true, Leaflet, too! Where is she now, do you know?"

"Yes. When our unit joined the Red Army, we handed her over to the farmers. Now she works on a collective farm."

So that is the story of Leaflet, the partisan horse.

Vitaly Volsky

A FRIEND IN NEED...

The sun was setting in the west, so I decided to return home from the forest park.

Expecting the forest to end soon, I left the winding path and struck across the woods in what I thought was the right direction. An hour passed, but the forest did not end. At first I thought I was passing through the same places as in the morning, but then I realised that I was in the wrong part of the forest. The trees had not been so tall, and I had not seen the fern undergrowth before.

"Did I lose my way?" I wondered in dismay.

My legs ached with exhaustion. I stopped, glanced at the sky and lay down under a tall and sprawling oak. The shadows were growing longer.

Woodpeckers were tapping all round and an oriole was whistling softly directly above me in the green foliage.

Suddenly, I heard a sharp low growl quite nearby. Then again.

I jumped to my feet. It sounded like a bear. That low growl was unmistakable.

Yet I knew that there were no bears in thereabouts. What could it be?

I walked towards the sound.

Then I saw a clearing ahead.

"Here comes the end of my wanderings!" I thought.

I walked faster and presently found myself in a forest clearing which was softly lit up by the evening sun. The whole clearing was thickly overgrown with bilberries. There seemed to be more ripe berries than green leaves on the little bushes.

A strange-looking, long and low structure loomed on the other side of the clearing. I came up closer and saw that my hearing had not deceived me.

I faced a cage containing live bears. The cage was divided into four long sections and joined by doors.

There was a bear in three of the sections. The fourth was empty.

A small house stood among tall pines about fifty metres from the cages.

A man came out of the house and approached me.

It was Matsuta, the forest ranger, who guarded the bears. He said it was about three kilometres to the hunters' lodge in Belovezha where I was staying at that time and invited me in.

We started to talk.

* * *

Forest ranger Matsuta lived there alone with the bears. He fed his shaggy charges and watched them.

"Aren't you lonely here?" I asked him.

"I don't have time to be lonely," answered Matsuta.

Then he told me the bears' story.

"Bears have not roamed free in Belovezhskaya Pushcha forest for about two hundred years. They've become extinct in these parts. So these bears had been brought here for breeding." The bears were peaceful and gentle. Before they arrived in Belovezhskaya Pushcha they had lived in zoos for a long time and one had even travelled with a circus. They were completely tame and had become so used to Matsuta that he walked freely into their cages.

Only one young female bear revealed an uneven temper. The forest smells aroused in her the instincts she inherited from free wild ancestors.

For days on end she stood with her snout thrust through the cage bars, and gulped in the clean, fresh forest air, obviously excited. But even she used to take food from the ranger's hand, and calmly allow him to enter the cage and to scratch her behind her ear.

But one morning, when the ranger approached the cage, he saw that it was empty. During the night the bear had gnawed through the wooden floor, dug a passage and escaped into the forest. That was in early June 1940. She thus began the life of a free animal.

Meanwhile, the sun had descended very low. The air became cooler. It was growing dark. I rose and bid Matsuta farewell.

The ranger walked with me to the road and pointed the way to Belovezha.

It was dark by the time I finally reached the lodge.

* * *

Even after I had arrived home I continued to think about the female bear. I asked about her my ranger friends and the local people.

The bear was seen often in different parts of the forest. For her, life was easy and carefree in the woods. There was enough food for a bear in the Pushcha. The bilberries, and wild strawberries transformed the green grass into a colourful carpet. There were raspberry growths taller than a man. Mushrooms grew everywhere. The bear found sweet roots in the ground, and tall juicy plants in the clearings.

Upon finding an ant-hill, she would dig into it, put in her front paws and slowly lick off the aroused ants who stubbornly and helplessly attacked their terrible enemy.

She would overturn rotten old stumps and always find lots of fat larvae, worms and snails in the black, damp soil underneath.

She would peel the bark off old trees with her long, sharp claws and find something to eat there too. Sometimes a young inexperienced wood grouse would become easy prey for the bear.

When the cold breath of autumn painted the forest yellow and red, the bear began to hunt for nuts and acorns.

She had fed very well in the summer and autumn. Preparing for winter, the bear had become plump and her fur shone with well-being.

When winter set in, the bear dug a lair where a tree had been uprooted in the thicket, in a place high enough to avoid the spring floods. The thicket was surrounded on all sides by a swamp overgrown with willows. Here she could feel completely safe from all enemies, protected from the cold winds and spring waters. She brought leaves, grass and moss to her lair.

46

In early December the bear settled down for the winter in her lair. Soon the lair was snowed under. The wind and blizzards howled over it, the trees crackled from the freezing cold but the bear felt nothing. Only the steam rising next to the uprooted tree showed that a living creature was sleeping under the snow.

* * *

In January 1941, during the winter hibernation, the bear gave birth to two cubs. They lay next to their mother in the lair, blind and helpless, sucking her milk for three months. Their eyes opened when they were four weeks old.

At the end of March, when the sun grew warm and the snow had melted, the bear left her lair. Lean and hungry, her fur hanging down in shreds, she began to roam the forests in search of food for herself and the growing cubs. When the cubs were born, they were no bigger than rats, but now they were the size of a small dog and demanded food all the time. The bear had eaten nothing all winter.

Some time later, when it was much warmer, the cubs began to leave the lair, too, but the mother didn't allow them to go far from their home.

In early May 1941, forest ranger Matsuta happened to come across the bear.

He was walking along low swampy land, which he rarely visited. It was a clear, sunny day.

He spotted the she-bear on a sand hill in the midst of a small forest swamp thickly overgrown with willows.

She lay on her side, front paws stretched out, basking in the sun.

"Why, that's our bear!" the forest ranger thought and came closer.

The she-bear was not alone. A little cub was playing nearby in the sand.

The cub would rise on its haunches and clamber on its mother's back or would do somersaults and play in the sand.

Another cub was about a dozen paces from its mother, trying to climb a tree. It had grasped the trunk with its paws, chest pressed firmly against it, and was trying very hard to make its way up the tree, letting out loud and irritated growls.

Apparently the mother bear was in a good mood. Sunning herself, she yawned frequently and screwed up her eyes.

One of the little cubs lay down to its mother.

The other would not abandon its attempt to climb the tall tree.

Matsuta stood and watched the happy family.

Suddenly the bear sensed danger. She lifted her head and began

48

sniffing the air. Then she got up, and took several steps towards Matsuta. Evidently the bear had sensed human presence.

Matsuta stood still.

His eyes met the animal's little eyes.

The bear stopped.

For a few minutes she stood still, her head raised, staring intently at Matsuta. Then, seemingly unalarmed, she turned and slowly crossed over with the cubs to the opposite side of the swamp.

A minute later they had disappeared in the thick willow growth.

"She must've recognised me, she wasn't afraid, even with the cubs there," Matsuta thought to himself.

* * *

Five years passed.

I didn't see forest ranger Matsuta again until 1945.

He told me the remarkable story of his last encounter with the bear.

During the Nazi occupation of Byelorussia, Matsuta served as a guide and scout for a partisan unit.

Once, on his way to a remote village in the western outskirts of Belovezhskaya Pushcha, he was ambushed by the Nazis and wounded in the left shoulder.

Escaping from the enemy, Matsuta ran for the forest and disappeared into the snow-filled thickets.

Unfamiliar with the terrain, the Nazis were afraid of going deep into the forest.

They fired their submachine guns after him, and turned back.

It was February and the end of the day. It was difficult for Matsuta to find his way in the dim light.

All was calm and quiet in the snow-covered forest.

Snowstorms had raged for a whole week, and everything was covered in deep snow.

At every step Matsuta sunk waist deep in snowdrifts.

He soon became exhausted. His wounded shoulder ached and his head spun.

His old worn coat offered little protection against the cold. Matsuta was soon frozen through. He felt his strength failing.

He could go no further, his last ounce of strength had gone and he dropped into a high snowdrift near an uprooted tree.

Suddenly, he felt the snow sinking under him, he was falling into a dark abyss and lost consciousness.

49

Matsuta came to in total darkness. He could see nothing but he felt warm. He was lying underground, on dry grass and leaves.

The air stank. The sharp smell of an animal hit his nose.

He could hear snorting and sighing in the darkness, the sound of smacking lips and growls.

"Where on earth am I?" wondered Matsuta.

Suddenly it flashed through his mind: "A lair! I must've fallen into a bear's lair!"

He lay there for a few minutes with his eyes open, staring into the darkness, then he began to feel around.

There was a low, dirt ceiling above him. His hand felt the thick and tangled roots of an old tree.

In front of him, from where he heard the smacking and growling, something warm, live and shaggy stirred and sighed.

"It must be my bear," thought Matsuta and at that moment his hand brushed a bear's shaggy head.

The forest ranger patted the bear and scratched behind her ear.

The smacking ceased immediately.

The bear lifted her head and sniffed the forest ranger. The next instant he felt the bear's tongue rough as sandpaper, lick his neck. Then she resumed her former position. The mistress of the lair had recognised her erstwhile guardian.

A fine knowledge of bear habits and two years' experience of living with them in the forest enabled Matsuta to behave correctly in this precarious situation. He lay very still, not allowing himself to move unnecessarily. He realised that the bear would not harm him without reason. She hadn't touched him when he had tumbled down unexpectedly into her lair. Now that the bear had acknowledged her former guardian, he had nothing to fear. He relaxed. His eyes gradually closed. He fell asleep, his head resting on the wide, warm side of the bear.

Matsuta had no idea of how long he'd slept there, in that warm lair. When he woke up, darkness reigned as before. He felt that his strength had returned and began to feel the walls and ceiling with his hands quietly to find a way out.

A blast of fresh air hit his face. A dim grey light broke into the lair from above. Matsuta braced his foot against a tangled root sticking out from the ground, and rose half way out of the lair.

Everything was still. The cold had relaxed. A light snowfall came from the grey morning sky.

Matsuta looked around for a few minutes. His lungs took in the cold bracing air, and he sighed with relief.

"Thanks, lassie!" the forest ranger mumbled and climbed out from the deep warm lair, where he had been given such a warm and hospitable welcome.

In the evening he was with his unit.

Maxim Luzhanin

YUZIK'S MOTHER GETS LOST

The August morning was as blue and clean as if it had been bathing in the lake's refreshing water. Yuzik and his mother were walking beside the lake. They had come here to spend their holiday.

People were standing, sitting and lying all over the sandy beach, there was no room to spread out their mat and put down the bags of food.

"Let's go to the children's beach. Only don't let go of my hand. You could get lost in no time at all. Then what would we do?"

His mother had repeated these words more than once, and Yuzik listened patiently, his hot and sweaty hand hanging on to his mother's fingers. Before long Yuzik saw something that looked like flowers in blossom: poppies, bluebells, buttercups. He had never seen such flowers and so many too. They were all running about, playing, singing and even wailing. Then he realised that this was the children's beach, and these were not flowers but children's heads in different-coloured caps.

Suddenly, Yuzik saw a butterfly net floating in front of his eyes. In it was an enormous butterfly which seemed to be made of golden velvet. How could he keep still? Yuzik's hand slipped from his mother's and he ran after the net.

But the net moved further away for the girl carrying it was also running. Yuzik had almost caught up with her, but she merged with a group of children and he lost sight of both her and the beautiful butterfly. To make matters worse, he couldn't see his mother anywhere either! No, he was not lost, Yuzik refused to even consider the possibility, it was his mother who was lost! The boy ran up and down the beach. Mother was nowhere to be seen.

Children were playing ball, skipping and splashing in the water. They all had their own little spot in this merry land of children—a mat spread out on the sand, or simply a newspaper, with a mother sitting on it. It's good to be under her watchful eye: you felt safe even if she seemed not looking.

Not that Yuzik was afraid to be alone. After all he was used to being independent in his back yard and in the kindergarten. He had even protected his mother once: he stood in front of an enormous dog as big as a calf and flung out his arms. And when Mother—wasn't she a scaredy-cat—had moaned and put her hands on her heart, he'd said calmly and seriously: "Don't worry, Mum, I won't hurt the doggie!"

Even now, as he was standing here she was probably trembling with fright. No! He'd better find her soon!

Sweating and gasping for breath Yuzik ran from one group of children to another: was his mother here? The grown-ups were sympathetic and asked him what his mother was wearing and what kind of hairstyle she had.

The questions and answers brought no results: there were lots of women in red frocks with white polka dots and fair hair bleached by the sun!

Yuzik was told to sit and rest for a while. He was offered sweets, buns and some people even poured him out a soft drink. The boy refused to accept anything: this was no time for treats! Mother was running about frantically somewhere, and, of course, calling for his help.

Then he had a brilliant idea. It was the only way he could find her: all the mothers were with children, but his mother was alone. So Yuzik began to walk along the shore again asking:

"Have you seen a woman without a little boy?"

People could not hold back a smile and recalled where they had actually seen such a woman. Soon Yuzik found his lost mother.

Both were overjoyed. But Mother did not show how worried she had been. Nor did Yuzik show how tired he was from looking for Mother on the beach.

Later, after a pleasant swim they ate a good lunch. Polishing off a hard-boiled egg with a tomato, Yuzik glanced at the glass of raspberry drink. He picked it up, but then gave it to Mother. Then, resting his head on that familiar tanned shoulder, he said reproachfully:

"Why don't you ever keep to the road? You could've got lost for good."

Pavel Kovalyov

WHEN TREES WEEP

I don't know if any of you have seen trees weeping. It was my grandfather Akhrem who showed me that trees wept.

It was in last October. I would probably never have noticed that the first freezing cold spell had struck the night before. But as soon as we left the house together that morning, Grandad Akhrem said:

"Well, Fedya, what do you see?"

I began looking carefully at everything. It all seemed untouched, thoughtful and silent. Only the sun seemed brighter to me. I told Grandad:

"The sun shines more."

"Uhu, yes." Grandad Akhrem agreed. "And what else? Take a better look."

I looked here and there, but didn't see anything unusual.

Grandad Akhrem gave a sly chuckle into his thick grey beard and lifted his eyes to the trees. I followed his glance. Something seemed to have changed during the night. And I said:

"There are more yellow leaves on the cherry trees."

Grandad smiled slyly. His eyes had a youthful twinkle. He looked first at one, then at another tree.

"Look closely," he said.

I looked at the cherry trees, at the young and tall poplar, which my father, a driver, brought from somewhere two or three years ago and planted in the street. And I said:

"The dew's dripping off the leaves of the poplar..."

"That's not dew, Fedya, they're tears," Grandad Akhrem explained.

I stared at Grandad.

"You see how it is, Fedya. Last night, the frost struck for the first time. See how the leaves have become darker on the trees."

"I see," I hurried with my reply so that Grandad would continue his story.

"These leaves were frozen. They were no longer soft. Then the sun shone, the ice melted..."

"And the trees are weeping," I could not resist putting in.

"Yes, the trees have started weeping."

"Will they weep for long?"

"Not for long now," Grandad sighed. "Soon the leaves will turn yellow and fall. Then snow will cover them."

Grandad approached the poplar and touched the wet leaves with his hand.

Then I noticed that Grandad Akhrem was no longer smiling. I suppose he too was sorry that the summer had ended so quickly.

Vasil Khomchenko

THREE HELMETS

Little Andrei has two helmets at home. They stand side by side on a shelf. One is a soldier's helmet; Grandfather brought it back from the war. That helmet saved his life. Grandfather was charging—he was not Grandfather then of course but a young man, a soldier—when a mine exploded in front of him. Splinters flew in every direction. One hit his helmet, knocking him to the ground. But the helmet was strong enough. Grandfather stayed alive.

The second one, his father's, is a peace-time helmet. Andrei's father is a foreman on a building site. He and his workers have built many blocks of flats, including the nine-storey one little Andrei lives in. Sometimes

Andrei goes through town with his father who points out: "That's my school. My community centre. I built your kindergarten too."

Father's helmet is a commemorative one. It's called a golden helmet. It is awarded to the best workers on the building site.

And so the two helmets stand side by side. Grandfather's is dark with dents made by bullets and splinters. Father's is a bright orange.

Andrei dreams of having his own helmet to wear when he grows up. He is sure it will be a cosmonaut's helmet. And, of course, Andrei will put it next to his father's and grandfather's. Then all three will stand side by side.

Pavel Misko

GRANDAD AND AL

While Grandma Nastya was in the pasture milking the cow, they returned from the barber's. Now both had the same haircut, a crew cut with a forelock. They were the same height now, although the grandfather was sixty and the grandson six years old.

Grandmother Natsya put a pail of milk on the bench and took off Grandfather's tank helmet. She always wore that helmet to milk the cow.

"Is that you, Al?" she rubbed the top of Grandfather's head. "I'll pour you some fresh milk."

"No! I'm Al!" the grandson laughed merrily. "But pour some milk for Grandad, too!"

Grandmother pretended not to believe him and rubbed Al's head.

"Yes, it is you all right. I wouldn't know you, my prickly little hedgehog!" she kissed her grandson's head and poured him a small cup and grandfather a large cup of milk. Both enjoyed their drink, grunted and wiped big white moustaches. Vaska the cat rubbed against their feet, his back arched and tail upwards; he also wanted some milk. Grandmother poured a little for him into a saucer.

"Would you like some more?" she asked.

"No, I've had enough. Well, we'll be off now!" said Al in a hurry.

"Where're you going? It's dinner-time!" said Grandma Nastya crossly.

"We're going to fish in the stream!" Al grabbed a glass jar with a string tied to it instead of a handle.

"Don't worry, we'll have dinner later, when we're really hungry," Grandfather Arkhip told Grandmother. "Where're my boots? Ah, there they are," he took the leather mittens from behind his belt and put them onto his wide calloused hands.

"Running off," sighed Grandma Nastya and put a chunk of bread into Grandfather's coat pocket.

Grandfather crawled out the door propelling himself with his hands.

"Grandad, are we taking the horsie?" said Al, waiting impatiently on the porch.

The horsie was a small cart on four ball-bearings. One sat on it and pushed with the hands. Grandfather also had a small car with a motor, real rubber tyres and a steering wheel.

"Yes, we are," said Grandad Arkhip.

He fastened the basket to his back. Al quickly rolled the horsie to the porch and put wooden "shoes" shaped like irons at each side.

Grandfather went down the steps on his hands, sat on the cart and took a "shoe" in each hand.

"Are you walking or riding?" asked Al for the umpteenth time.

"I'm flying," answered Grandfather seriously. Using the "shoes", he propelled himself forward.

By the time they had left the garden, Grandfather was breathing heavily. The path descended, the ball-bearings cut into the damp earth and got caught in the tall grass and plantain. Grandad Arkhip stopped, looked down at the meadow where the stream weaved in and out the alder bushes, and sighed.

"It would be easier to go on foot from here," he decided and climbed off the horsie. He put it sideways into the thick grass and left the "shoes" there, too. "Come on, take off your sandals!" he said to Al.

There was no need to persuade the boy. He had his sandals and socks off in a jiffy. Grandad fastened the sandals onto his belt and put the socks into his pocket.

"Right, let's run!"

Al either rushed ahead down the path or circled round Grandad, getting entangled in the tall grass, falling and laughing. Frightened butterflies fluttered away, fanning themselves with their wings — it was so hot! Bees buzzed busily and the fat yellow and black bumble-bees droned somnolently.

"Grandad, you're like a tortoise with that basket," shouted Al.

Grandad did not answer. He stopped to rest, dangled his wrists and breathed heavily. But he looked around with clear, smiling eyes.

"Run, run," he sighed. "The grass tickles the soles of your feet, doesn't it? And clover flowers get caught between your toes. That happened to me, too. It would be a flower and a toe, a flower and a toe. They prick your toes, don't they?" Grandad's smile was sad now. "Closer to the stream, the water seeps from underneath your feet. It seems dry, but when you put your foot down, the water seeps through. And it's cold..."

Grandad Arkhip walked some more on his hands and stopped again.

"If you only knew how wonderful it is to walk on dew! You'd never have a cold, if you walked on dew. I used to be a herdsman, and I'd follow the herd barefoot, dewdrops as big as beans. And so clean. And the sun shone in every drop. My soles would feel cold, but after I'd run a bit they'd start burning. And in the daytime the dry coarse grass made my feet sore. You couldn't know about these things! I'd run to the foot-bridge where the butterflies and dragonflies, big blue ones and reddish ones, were perched in the sun. 'Don't be afraid, there's plenty of room for all of us!' I'd say. But they'd flutter away. I'd sit on a warm log and put my feet in the water. Ah, it was sheer bliss. I'd dangle my feet, and they'd no longer feel sore. I'd even doze off. The sun played hide-and-seek with the water. The small fry would swim up to my feet and tickle them with their lips. I'd move my toes, and they'd rush off like spray. The cool water would caress my feet, sheer bliss."

Grandad pattered over the ground with his leather gloves.

At last they reached the stream. The water was ankle-deep, knee-deep at most. If one looked closely one could see the small fish and all kinds of bugs. And there were so many water plants, the sedge sticking out like sharp sabres!

"Well, here we are," said Grandad unfastening the basket. "Come on, take a dip in the water. And I'll walk along the bank and carry your fish." He took the jar from Al's hands, crawled closer to the water and scooped some water into it.

At first Al was hesitant about going into the water, but Grandad urged him on:

"Feel the water with your foot, don't be afraid. It'll seem cold at first, afterwards you won't want to get out. You'll splash and splash. Can you feel the pebbles on the bottom? The gravel's hard, it even crunches. Sometimes

you come across silt, it's slushy and the foot sinks into it. Once I felt something move under my toes. I grabbed it with my hand—a tench this big!" Grandad showed his palm. "Or the slime gets hold of your foot, it's slushy and slippery. Be careful when you put your foot down, there might be a sharp snag there. Lower the basket carefully into the water, at an angle to the bank. Now, splash with your foot, drive the fish in and lift it fast!"

"I've got it!" Al shouted at the top of his voice and rushed onto the bank.

The old man and the little boy grabbed at the slippery and quick gudgeons. They cried out and laughed—both were so happy.

They only-started back home when the sun was already in the west, but still warmed their crewcuts. Al was chewing on the chunk of bread which Grandad had found—by pure chance—in his pocket.

"Don't hurry. Chew it a long time and keep it in your mouth. Doesn't the bread seem to become sweet? As if it has sugar in it," said Grandad.

"Aha," Al chewed hurriedly. "I never thought that bread could be so delicious. Ordinary rye bread!"

Al carried his catch in the jar—a few dozen gudgeons. As he went along he imagined how his grandmother and he would meet the cow when the herd came back from pasture, and how he'd run into the house to get the tank helmet. On the way to the shed he'd try it on himself. It's a bit big. Grandad's size, he had fought in it. But it's just right for Grandma, she looks like a real tankman in it—and isn't afraid of the cow hitting her head with her tail.

Grandad found the horsie in the grass.

"Do you want to put your sandals on?" he asked his grandson.

"No, I'm going to toughen up!" Al replied.

Grandad sat on the cart supporting himself with what was left of his legs. It is even more difficult to go uphill on the horsie. The ball-bearings squeaked although they've been oiled.

The first to run out of the gates was Vaska the cat, hoping to be treated to some fish. Grandma Nastya was standing by the porch, smiling at them. She was taking the clothes she had hung out for airing off the line. She carefully picked up grandfather's tunic which was heavy under the weight of medals. Al heard them jingle and saw the sunlight reflected in them.

Ales Shashkov

HOW NICK NOODLE BECAME A GENERAL

There were four of us: Len Grom, Pete Gruk and I—Dima Veres—and Nick Noodle, whose real name was Vasya Radkevich. But we always called Vasya names, because he was so quiet with big dark eyes that blinked meekly. He did not object, because he knew that he would get ten days of extra duty if he did. You see, all three of us were his commanders.

And Nick Noodle was a private. He was the one who would fall into line and charge behind General Len Grom, storming one fortress after another. He would be followed by the fat Pete Gruk, our Chief of Staff, breathing heavily and rolling ahead like a tank. Then came I, the division commissar. We would charge straight into the enemy trenches, throwing plastic bottles of water and imagining enemy soldiers getting killed with our grenades.

After each engagement we would return to base, line up and Len Grom would pin military awards—different-coloured badges—on the officers' chests.

Private Noodle would stand dumbly. Receiving a minor decoration, in the shape of a plastic button, he would say "Again?" and ask hopelessly, if not for a real mark of distinction, at least for the rank of corporal.

This would probably have gone on for a long time had it not been for something that happened.

On that quiet sunny day we were assaulting enemy fortifications on the other side of our river. Nick Noodle was helping his father repair the roof, and so we had no one to command. So Len Grom sighed deeply and declared:

"I'll go on reconnaissance mission myself. When you hear an owl hooting, swim to the other side right away."

Len undressed reluctantly and, drawing his head into his shoulders, dropped into the water with such a splash that the geese honked in fright on the enemy bank.

Pete and I lay down in the grass and watched our commander. But all we could see were his hands in the golden splashes of water.

Suddenly Len's arms stopped flashing, he craned his neck as if he wanted to issue a new order and disappeared under water.

"He's fathoming the depth," said Pete knowledgeably.

Then Len reappeared, waved his arms and we clearly heard his desperate cry of "Help!"

In panic, we ran along the bank calling to him. Len no longer cried for help. He would appear for an instant, then disappear in the water again.

That was when we saw Noodle. He came at a run and, fully dressed, dived into the water. Swiftly and surely, he swam towards the place we had last seen our commander's head.

Terrified that Nick would also perish, Pete and I ran away.

We learned what happened afterwards at Len's house. Noodle had saved Len, who soon recovered and appeared at base again. He ordered glumly:

"To the positions, march!"

Our eyes lowered, we followed our commander half-heartedly. My ears burned with shame, while Pete sniffed and looked down at his shoes covered in dust.

Seeing us from a distance, Noodle came running and stood at attention as usual.

"At ease," Len said, waving his hand and, turning towards us, said grimly: "Now Vasya Radkevich is our commander. And we're his soldiers. Is that clear? 'Shun!"

Once again we stormed enemy fortresses, captured pill boxes and machine-gun nests, crossed rivers. But now we were commanded by Nick Noodle, our new general. He pinned medals on our chests and we thanked him. We did not even dare to ask for the rank of corporal.

Vladimir Lipsky

A NEW GAME

Sunday is Marina's favourite day. Mummy and Daddy don't work on that day, so she doesn't have to go to the kindergarten.

All of Marina's friends play in the backyard of the house. There are swings, a sand box, tables and benches in the playground.

Once the girls get together it's impossible to separate them. They feed and dress their dolls, sing lullabies and invent new games.

One day Marina went into the playground with an enormous teddy bear rather than her dolls. His ears stuck out in a funny way, and his dark eyes shone. You could see the red tip of his tongue in his mouth. When you touched the bear he began to mumble: no one knew whether he was talking, or complaining to his mistress.

"Show us your bear!" the children cried out.

Marina pressed the bear to her chest and said:

"He mustn't be bothered; he's tired. He's travelled all the way from the BAM." *

"Where's that?" asked Lena.

"Daddy says it's a wonderful land, a very long way from here. It has wild forests, lots of snow and it's freezing cold. Real bears live there."

"Did your teddy bear live in the forest, too?" inquired little Sveta.

"No, Daddy bought him in a shop, but he did see a real bear once. It came to the house in which Daddy slept."

Marina sat down on a bench. The girls were sitting and standing around her. Everyone wanted to pat the teddy bear from the BAM.

Marina remembered what her father had told her and in her own words she passed it on to her friends:

"No one lived in that land before. Then it became known that there was a huge treasure there. Brave people went there to build a railway across swift rivers, swamps, forests and rocky mountains. They were not afraid of the freezing cold, the bears or the dark forest."

"Why are they building the railway?" asked Tanya.

"To carry out the treasure which everyone needs," answered Marina.

"Do we need it, too?" Vera asked in surprise.

"Father said that the treasure can be used to build new towns and make lots of toys and pretty clothes."

"And teddy bears like yours?"

"And teddy bears as well," Marina said after pondering, and patted the BAM bear.

"Oh, I love new toys!" said little Sveta.

On that day the children in our block invented a new game.

Singing the song "We're building a railway" they built a sandy road. Toy trucks rolled along the road to the mysterious BAM treasures.

The dolls sat on the bench. There was no one to put them to bed that day.

---

* BAM is the short for the Baikal-Amur Railway, a new construction project in East Siberia.

Dair Slavkovich

FLOWERS IN THE POSTBOX

Nastya met the postwoman at the gate and took the newspaper.

The postwoman wiped the perspiration from her brow.

"Aunt Marina, don't you find it hard carrying such a heavy bag?"

"And how! See for yourself."

"Why do you have so many newspapers?"

"Because people subscribe to many. They read a lot so that they'll know more."

"May I help you?"

"How can you help me, dear girl? The bag's too heavy for your shoulders."

"I'll walk along the street with you. You'll take a newspaper to one house, I'll take a newspaper to another. We'll do the job faster, and then it'll be easier for you."

"Don't go to all that trouble, it'll tire your legs."

"It's nothing."

So they went along together. Aunt Marina went to one house, Nastya to another.

They covered the rounds of the whole township in just half an hour. It was fast and efficient. There was only one problem: the postboxes were so high in three of the houses that Nastya couldn't reach them.

"You've been such a great help," said Aunt Marina when they were parting. "Thank you, my assistant."

From then on Nastya went to the other end of the town every day. She would meet Aunt Marina at the bridge.

The people began to call Nastya postgirl. She liked that very much.

"Is there only a newspaper for me today?" they asked in one house.

"Only a newspaper, but it's a very interesting one," she answered.

"Any letters, Nastya?" they asked in another house.

"They're still writing them," Nastya joked like Aunt Marina.

She was very warmly welcomed by the old lady teacher. The postgirl enjoyed dropping in at her house.

But, on Monday they had nothing to deliver to the old lady.

"Aunt Marina, why aren't we taking anything to the teacher?"

"Her newspaper doesn't come out on Monday. And there are no letters or magazines for her."

Nastya felt sorry for the old lady:

"She's probably sitting and brooding: 'The postgirl has not come today. Must've felt lazy.' Perhaps..." she gave a start at the unexpected thought.

When they'd finished with the post and Aunt Marina went back, Nastya ran out of the town into a field where the flax blossomed and wheat grew.

There were plenty of flowers just for the picking there!

On that day the teacher found a bouquet of wild daisies and cornflowers in her postbox. The teacher took the flowers out of the box carefully and lifted them to her face. And her face lost its wrinkles, looked youthful and broke out in a happy smile.

Mikola Gil

WE CAN SEE THE SUN

He was a soldier.

He became a soldier in 1941 when the Nazis invaded his country.

He was not an ordinary soldier. He was an engineer. Soldiering is a difficult job for any man, but for an engineer it is even more dangerous and difficult. That is because a military engineer is always in front, where it is hardest. The engineers go first to the places where the tanks are to advance followed by infantry. Their job is to remove enemy mines.

An engineer must be brave. He must also have nerves of steel and skilful hands. This is because if the engineer's hands tremble you can count him lost: a mine will explode in trembling hands. The engineer must not make mistakes. No wonder they say that an engineer makes only one mistake in his life. And that mistake costs him his life.

He was brave, our soldier, he had nerves of steel and skilful hands. He never made mistakes. He rendered harmless hundreds, maybe even thousands, of mines and cleared the way for victory. It was a long way indeed. It took four years and ended on May 9, 1945.

The soldier thought his service had ended. He came home hoping to plough the land, mow the grass and harvest grain. But there was tragedy at home. His teenage son was killed by a land mine left behind by the enemies. He had seen death many times during the war, but his hair turned grey at thirty three when his son died.

Once he learned about a whole ward of teenagers injured by mines. It was called the "miners' ward". It was a bitter joke. The soldier visited the ward. He was just as distressed as he had been by his son's death. In particular, he remembered a boy who had empty eye-sockets instead of eyes. The boy's words were forever imprinted on the soldier's mind: "Mister, I can't see the sun..."

So the soldier donned his military uniform again. And he continued to clear the land of Nazi mines, shells and bombs. Every time he defused another mine he cast it aside in disgust as if it were a dead poisonous snake and murmured: "Now you'll never shut away the sun from anyone."

The soldier continued to do his dangerous and noble work for many years so that people and animals could walk freely and children could play wherever they wanted.

There were wars in other countries too. War raged for many years in distant Africa, on Algeria's arid land. And mines, bombs and shells also remained there, killing people, animals and birds, and there were also "miners' wards".

When the Algerian government asked the Soviet Union to help clear the land of the terrible seeds of war, the soldier boarded a ship and sailed there. Because he was a Soviet soldier, the friend and protector of all honest people on earth.

He had never made a mistake, our soldier. His hands never trembled. He rendered harmless thousands of mines and shells. And in distant Algeria, discarding a poisonous snake deprived of its venom, he said as he had in his own country: "Now you'll never shut the sun away from anyone."

He remembered one small village in Algeria for the rest of his life. All the villagers welcomed the Soviet soldier. He remembered a girl, who presented him with a bouquet of wild flowers. The girl was dark-skinned, almost black, and her smile lit up the whole of her round face. He had to demine a field which was already overgrown with grass in that village. The peasants had tried to plough up the field but several of them never returned from their work. Now the peasants expected the Soviet soldier to return their field to them. And the dark-skinned girl presented him with some wild flowers.

He had almost cleared the field. There was only a small patch left to do. But the soldier was tired.

That evening an explosion rocked the village. The peasants knew what had happened. They brought the Soviet soldier into the village. He was alive but the sun had been shut away from him for ever. He heard and felt the hot Algerian sun but couldn't see it.

No wonder they say an engineer makes only one mistake.

Thousands of people came to see him off. The dark-skinned girl presented him with another bouquet of flowers, and although he could not see her, he recognised her and his strong hand stroked her coarse hair. It must have been the first time his hand trembled.

At home he learned that he had become a grandfather. His daughter had given birth to a girl. His granddaughter was fair-haired with blue eyes, but to his family's amazement he always called her Darkie. Perhaps it was because the last girl he saw, or would ever see, was that dark-skinned Algerian girl with the radiant smile.

We can all see the sun. You can see it and I can see it. But there is a tall, grey-haired man walking down our quiet street, feeling the way with a cane. He is a former soldier, a former military engineer.

The sun shines into his face, but he cannot see the sun.

Let us bow low in gratitude to that man!

Pavel Tkachev

INSTRUCTIONS

In the morning Vladimir Lenin conducted a session of the Council of Labour and Defence.* It took longer than expected. After the session Lenin went straight to a workers' meeting at a Moscow factory. Several days earlier the workers had invited Lenin to speak to them.

When he returned, Lenin hardly had time to reach his office when the telephone operator reported:

"The Commander of the Western Front is on the phone."

Lenin inquired about everything: did they have the necessary arms and ammunition, what was the situation with food and uniforms. Finally, he said:

"Above all, take care of the men."

---

* The story is set in 1918, the period of the Civil War in Russia.

Then, delegates from the peasants arrived led by an old man with a grey beard.

"Please come in, comrades. Be seated," Lenin invited them.

"Begging your pardon, we'll stand," answered the grey-bearded peasant.

"Why? Legs tire easily, isn't that so?" Lenin addressed the peasants.

They all laughed and sat down on the chairs.

The old man opened up the conversation. His name was Ivan Andreyevich.

"We've come to complain about our village Soviet, Vladimir Ilyich. We prepared bricks for a new church and they took them away..."

"Took them away? Do you need a new church so badly?"

"Well, I don't know quite how to put it..."

"Just say what you think."

"The old folk have to pray somewhere, but the young don't go to church. They want books."

"You see, they want books. You do have a church, even if an old one, but there's no school, is there?"

"That's true, of course..."

At the end of the talk it was decided: Lenin would order the Soviet to return the bricks to the peasants, while the peasants would build both a new church and a school.

Lenin warmly said good-bye to the peasants.

Then Krzhizhanovsky dropped in to discuss questions of the country's electrification. Only after four p.m. did Vladimir Ilyich sit down at his desk. He wrote in an even handwriting:

"Today I would like to discuss the basic tasks of the Young Communist League..." Lenin stopped writing. He took his eyes off the paper and began to think. The word "young" brought back memories of his own childhood and school years. He was returning home from high school. He ran merrily into the hall. The door to his father's study was open, Ilya Nikolayevich was working. Passing the study, Vladimir gave a quick report: "Greek excellent! German excellent! Algebra excellent!"

His father was pleased.

"Algebra excellent!" Lenin said aloud and laughed. "No, my voice has changed."

He rose from his chair, walked up to the window where there was a large green palm tree in a tub. One leaf had turned yellow. Lenin walked around the palm and looked out of the window. Through the window he could see the Trinity Tower and the Kremlin yard. The tower was built to last for centuries. Lenin admired its beauty, the beauty of the autumn day and did not hear his secretary come in.

"Excuse me, Vladimir Ilyich, the mail."

"Please put it on the desk, Lidia Alexandrovna, I'll attend to it in a moment," said Lenin, without turning away from the window.

It seemed that Lenin had forgotten about everything. Affairs of state had faded into the background. He seemed fascinated by the magnificent tower. But this was not so. Although Lenin was looking at the tower, he was actually thinking about the subject of his speech to the YCL congress, which he had begun to work on. It was about the tasks facing young communists. It was up to today's young boys and girls to complete the task which their elders had begun in 1917, and to build communism. And success depended on...

A knock came at the door. The secretary came in again.

"Vladimir Ilyich, Nadezhda Konstantinovna* called: dinner is ready."

"Dinner?" Lenin exclaimed in surprise and took out his watch. It was past four. He asked Lidia Alexandrovna: "Please tell her I'll be there soon, I'm coming now."

Stopping by his desk Lenin examined his mail. His attention was drawn to a big grey envelope. The handwriting was that of a child: "Moscow, Grandfather Vladimir Ilyich Lenin."

A bit lower he read:

"From Vasil Adamchik in Mogilev Gubernia."

Lenin smiled and took the envelope and the newspaper *Pravda* with him.

"If anything crops up, call me at my flat," he asked Lidia Alexandrovna.

There were a few spare minutes after dinner. Lenin opened the newspaper and moved the chair to the window: it was rather dark in the room. But then he remembered the letter and put the newspaper aside. He opened the envelope carefully with scissors and took out a letter and a drawing. It showed a dashing horseman brandishing a sword. Enemies were fleeing before him. There was no hope for them. In another instant the sword would reach them.

The caption read: "Lenin the Dashing Knight."

"Nadya," Lenin called Nadezhda Konstantinovna. "Look! I'm a knight!"

Lenin laughed out loud. Nadezhda Konstantinovna looked at the drawing and also laughed. Then she said:

"This artist has ability. He should study."

"Yes, study..."

"Where's he from?" Nadezhda Konstantinovna picked up the envelope. "It only has the district on it. There's no full address."

"Maybe he's written his address in the letter?" Lenin opened the letter

---

* Nadezhda Konstantinovna Krupskaya—Lenin's wife and associate.

and began to read:

"Dear Grandfather Lenin! This letter is being written by Vasil Adamchik from Mogilev Gubernia. First of all, my mother Anna, the peasants of our village and I want to send you our best wishes. I have also enclosed a picture. My mother says it's very good. Chairman of the Soviet Uncle Stepan and his wife, Aunt Avdotya, also liked the picture. Uncle Stepan even praised me. He said: 'Well done, Vasil. You got Lenin just right in your picture.'

"Uncle Stepan would know because he saw you himself. It was in Petrograd. You spoke from the top of an armoured car.

"I wanted to draw a picture like that, but I've never seen an armoured car.

"Dear Grandfather Lenin, please send a letter to Uncle Stepan that he will sign me up for the Red Army. I want to fight the rich. There are rumours in the village that the local squire Lisnianski will soon return. He'll take away the land, burn my books and pencils and make me tend his pigs.

"I asked Uncle Stepan, but he says: 'You have to grow up first, it's time now for you to study. Soon we'll open a school and you can fight your books there.' Please write to our chairman Uncle Stepan so that I can join the Red Army.

"Best wishes to you, Grandfather Lenin!

"Vasil Adamchik."

Lenin finished reading the letter and said:

"Chairman Stepan's right: it's the time for young people to fight books. It's shame there's no address. Nadya, I must go."

In his study Lenin sat at his desk and continued writing.

The light in Lenin's study was on for a long time. Lenin was preparing instructions for the Byelorussian boy Vasil, for millions of boys and girls like him, for their elder brothers and sisters, for all future generations:

"The task of the youth in general, and of the Young Communist Leagues and all other organisations in particular, might be summed up in a single word: learn."

REQUEST TO READERS

Raduga Publishers would be glad to have your opinion of this book, its translation and design and any suggestions you may have for future publications.

Please send all your comments to 17, Zubovsky Boulevard, Moscow, USSR.

ИБ № 1862

Редактор русского текста Г. И. Дзюбенко
Контрольный редактор Р. С. Боброва
Художник М. М. Краковский
Художественный редактор Н.·Н. Щербакова
Технический редактор О. Н. Черкасова

Сдано в набор 5.06.84. Подписано в печать 22.04.85. Формат 70x90/16. Бумага офсетная.
Гарнитура Таймс. Печать офсет. Условн. печ. л. 6,44. Усл. кр.-отт. 27,79. Уч.-изд. л. 6,43.
Тираж 17260 экз. Заказ № 3726 Цена 90 к. Изд. № 979.

Издательство ''Радуга'' Государственного комитета СССР по делам издательств, полиграфии
и книжной торговли. Москва, 119859, Зубовский бульвар, 17.

Ленинградская фабрика офсетной печати № 1 Союзполиграфпрома при Государственном
комитете СССР по делам издательств, полиграфии и книжной торговли.
Ленинград, 197101, ул. Мира, 3.